Aunt Matilda

Uncle Maximus

USING THIS BOOK

*One of the best ways of helping children to learn to read is by reading stories to them and with them. This way they learn what **reading** is, and they will gradually come to recognise many words, and begin to read for themselves.*

First, grown-ups read the story on the left-hand pages aloud to the child.

You can reread the story as often as the child enjoys hearing it. Talk about the pictures as you go.

Later the child will read the words under the pictures on the right-hand page.

The pages at the back of the book will give you some ideas for helping your child to read.

British Library Cataloguing in Publication Data
McCullagh, Sheila K.
    The Wideawake Mice. — (Puddle Lane. Series no. 855. Stage 1; v. 6)
    I. Title   II. Theobalds, Prue   III. Series
    428.6   PR6063.A165/
    ISBN 0-7214-0919-9

First edition

© Text and layout SHEILA McCULLAGH MCMLXXXV
© In publication LADYBIRD BOOKS LTD MCMLXXXV

The Wideawake Mice

written by SHEILA McCULLAGH
illustrated by PRUE THEOBALDS

This book belongs to:

CLAIRE MILNE.

Ladybird Books Loughborough

Mr Wideawake kept a toy shop
in Candletown.
(The toy shop wasn't far
from Puddle Lane.)
There were all kinds of toys
in the shop.
There were toy soldiers and castles,
and a big red kite.
There were dolls and boats
and a beautiful rocking horse.
And there was a large, greeny-brown egg.

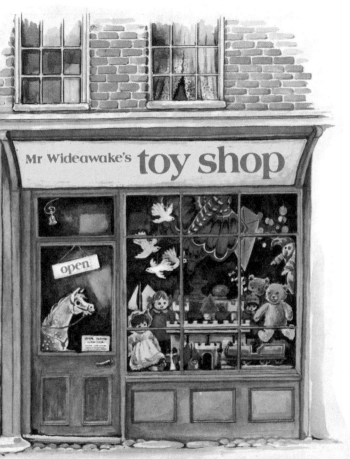

Mr Wideawake's toy shop

Mr Wideawake's
toy shop

A family of toy mice stood
on a shelf in the toy shop,
just under the counter
where Mr Wideawake took the money.

There was Grandmother Mouse
and Grandfather Mouse.

Grandmother Mouse
and
Grandfather Mouse

There was Uncle Maximus,
and Aunt Matilda.
(Father Mouse and Mother Mouse
had been sold before Christmas.)

Uncle Maximus and Aunt Matilda

There were two mouse children.
They were called Jeremy Mouse
and Miranda Mouse.

Jeremy Mouse
Miranda Mouse

And then there was Aunt Jane.
Jeremy and Miranda liked
to look at Aunt Jane.
She looked so cheerful, and
she looked so alive.
But they couldn't say anything to her.
They couldn't even move next to her.
They were all toy mice,
standing on the shelf, and
there was nothing they could do
but stand there.
And then, one day, something happened
which changed everything.

Aunt Jane

The day was almost over.
It was evening, and
it was getting dark in the shop.
Mr Wideawake had just lit a lamp,
when the door of the shop opened,
and an old man came in.
He had white hair, and
very bright blue eyes.
Mr Wideawake didn't know it,
but the old man was a magician.
The Magician lived
in the old house
at the end of Puddle Lane.

the Magician

"Good evening," said Mr Wideawake.
"What can I do for you?"
The Magician pointed to
the large, greeny-brown egg,
which was on the counter.
"I should like to buy that,"
he said.

the egg

Mr Wideawake didn't really want
to sell the egg.

"The egg costs a lot of money," he said.

"You don't know who might be inside it.

It's very expensive.

Why not buy a mouse instead?"

"I'll take the egg," said the Magician.

He said it so firmly, that
Mr Wideawake didn't say any more.

He picked up the egg,
and made it into a parcel.

Mr Wideawake
picked up the egg.

The Magician put his hand
into his pocket.
But when he pulled out his purse,
he pulled out a little box, too.
It was a beautiful silver box,
and it was full of silver dust.
As the Magician pulled out the box,
the lid came open, and
a little silver dust spilled out.

The Magician
pulled out a
little silver box.

The dust floated downwards.
It fell on the family of toy mice.

The magic dust fell on
the toy mice.

The Magician pushed the lid back
on the box.
He didn't see the magic dust
which had fallen out.
He put the box back in his pocket.
He paid for the egg,
picked up the parcel,
and went out of the shop.

The Magician went out
of the shop.

Somewhere outside, a clock struck six.

"Six o'clock!" said Mr Wideawake.
"It's time for tea."
Mr Wideawake lived over his shop.
He locked the door,
and he picked up the lamp.
He left the shop,
and went upstairs for his tea.
He didn't even glance at the family
of little mice.

Mr Wideawake
left the shop.

It was very dark and still
in the toy shop,
after Mr Wideawake had gone.
For some time, nothing happened.
And then the moon shone in
through the window.
It shone on the family of little mice.
As the moon shone on the magic dust,
the magic dust began to shine.

The moon shone on
the toy mice.
The moon shone on
the magic dust.

Grandfather Mouse stirred.

He shook the magic dust from his head,
and took a step forward.

"I can move!" he cried.

"I can talk, too!"

"So can I!" said Grandmother Mouse.

(She sounded very surprised.)

Grandfather Mouse
and
Grandmother Mouse

"I can move, too," said Jeremy Mouse.

"I can talk," said Miranda.

Jeremy and Miranda

"We can all talk," said Aunt Jane.
"We can all move.
The Magician's dust was magic.
It has made us come to life."
"What shall we do?"
asked Grandmother Mouse.
"We can't go on standing here,
now we're alive."

Aunt Jane and
Grandmother Mouse

"We'll go away!" said Grandfather Mouse.
"We'll go off somewhere,
and find a house of our own."
"Don't leave us behind!"
cried Uncle Maximus.
"Of course we shan't leave you,"
said Grandfather Mouse.
"We shall all go together."
He got down from the shelf,
and on to the floor.

Grandfather Mouse
got down.

Aunt Jane saw a hole.

"Look!" she said.

"There's a hole under the door.
We could get through that."
They all climbed down
after Grandfather Mouse,
and went over to the hole.
Aunt Jane crept through the hole first,
and Miranda and Jeremy followed.

Aunt Jane saw a hole.

Then Grandmother Mouse went
through the hole.
Aunt Matilda crept through very carefully,
so as not to tear her dress.
Uncle Maximus hurried after her.
He didn't want to be left behind.
It was a very tight fit
for Uncle Maximus.
He was a very large mouse, and
he had to take his coat off
to get through.
Even then, he almost got stuck.
But Grandfather pushed
and Aunt Jane pulled, and
at last Uncle Maximus got out.
Then Grandfather Mouse followed him.

Aunt Jane pulled, and
Uncle Maximus got out.

When Mr Wideawake came down
into the shop next morning,
the shelf was empty.
The mice had gone.
"Burglars!" cried Mr Wideawake,
looking at the empty shelf.
"Someone has stolen my mice!"
But the door was locked,
and no one had broken the window.
"I must have sold them,
and forgotten all about it,"
said Mr Wideawake.

Mr Wideawake
in the shop

Notes for the parent/teacher

Turn back to the beginning, and print the child's name in the space on the title page, using ordinary, not capital letters.

Now go through the book again. Look at each picture and talk about it. Point to the caption below, and read it aloud yourself.

Run your finger along under the words as you read, so that the child learns that reading goes from left to right.

Encourage the child to read the words under the illustrations. Don't rush in with the word before he/she has had time to think, but don't leave him/her floundering.

Read this story as often as the child likes hearing it. The more opportunities he/she has of looking at the illustrations and **reading** the captions with you, the more he/she will come to recognise the words.

If you have several books, let the child choose which story he/she would like.

Mrs Pitter... dropped the tail with a ...
She made such a noise,
that she woke Mr Gotobed,
who was fast asleep in bed
in the house at the end
of the lane.

Mr Gotobed woke up.